The world around the corner

The world around the corner

Maurice Gee

Oxford University Press

Wellington Oxford New York

Oxford University Press
222-36 Willis Street, Wellington

Oxford   London   Glasgow
New York   Toronto   Melbourne   Wellington
Kuala Lumpur   Singapore   Hong Kong   Tokyo
Nairobi   Dar es Salaam   Cape Town
Delhi   Bombay   Calcutta   Madras   Karachi

ISBN 0 19 558061 3

Designed by Lindsay Missen
Illustrations by Gary Hebley

Photoset in Garamond by Whitcoulls Ltd,
Christchurch, New Zealand
Printed in Hong Kong by Brighter Printing Press Ltd.

Contents

Chapter one: The secondhand shop   1

Chapter two: The mattress loft   11

Chapter three: The hut in the old-man's-beard   18

Chapter four: Auction day   23

Chapter five: The world of Sun and Moon   33

Chapter six: Beetle, rat, cat   43

Chapter seven: Grimbles!   50

Chapter eight: Moon-girl   58

Chapter nine: Caroline's dream   67

For Emily

The secondhand shop

Caroline stood in the summer rain with her head thrown back and her arms wide. She loved these storms that came out of a black sky, loved the raindrops large as sparrows' eggs and warm as tea. They splashed on her cheeks and her open hands. She caught them in her mouth. It was like being in some magic land, she thought, where rain was warm, and the trees had voices and the mountains went down into the ground instead of into the sky. Then a roaring on the iron roofs of the town warned her the storm was coming and she ran for cover over the dusty yard into the back door of her father's shop. She dried her cheeks with her handkerchief. A raindrop had splashed on her glasses. Half the world looked as if it was swimming. She took them off and polished them. Sometimes she hated her glasses. They kept on getting in the way. But at least, she thought, they had stopped the rain from coming down into her eye.

She had worn glasses since she was four. One day at breakfast she had said, 'Why have I got two plates of porridge?'

'Don't be silly, Caroline,' her mother said.

'I've got two Mummies too, and two Daddies.'

Her mother took her off to the doctor at once, and the doctor sent her to a specialist, who put her in hospital and did an operation on her eyes – like straightening the headlights of a car, he explained. When she came out she had to wear glasses. She did not like that. It meant she could not stay out in the rain, or stay in the water too long at the beach, and she had to be very careful playing games. The glasses cost a lot of money and her parents could not afford a new pair if they were broken. But there were good things too. Twigs no longer poked her in the eyes. That was a help when she climbed the tree after plums or crawled through tunnels in the old-man's-beard. And she could use the lenses as burning glasses. She had tried burning her initials into her ruler. But by the time she had the C done she saw two rulers and that scared her. She was careful to keep her glasses on after that. Now, after four years, she noticed them only at times like this, when rain splashed on the lenses.

She stood at the back door of her father's shop watching the drops make moon-craters in the yard, and vanish down cracks in the earth. It had been a dry summer. Then she turned and wandered back into the shop. Her father was in the little glass office, bent over his accounts. He smiled as she wandered by but she saw he did not want to be disturbed. She walked very carefully. This was the expensive part of the shop. It was filled with old and beautiful things, made of brass and crystal and coloured glass and wood with grain like waves in the sea or clouds in the sky. She loved them but they frightened her. Her father said if she broke or scratched anything here his profit for a month would be gone, they would have to start living on baked beans.

She walked along the narrow pathways through the antiques like someone in a jungle filled with brightly-coloured poisonous snakes. There were *chaises* and chiffoniers – she loved saying those foreign names – and ewer sets, and pewter beer-mugs, and chamber pots, and fairy chandeliers with glass lusters that sparkled like diamonds, and candlesticks, and old brass guns, and a harpsichord, and a suit of armour, and Royal Doulton plates, and an Indian god called Shiva, and a brass spy-glass, and many more things, many many more, all beautiful or bright or interesting – and all terribly expensive. She held her skirt in close to her body. Coming back past the office she smiled at her father, and he winked at her. He was, she thought, like a pirate sitting in his cave of treasures.

She walked down the shop past an old woman peering at some willow-pattern plates – her father was secretly keeping an eye on her – and went between a chiffonier and a *chaise* ('chiffonier,' she whispered, 'chaise') and through a curtain of hanging beads into the other part of the building, the tatty part, where her father sold junk and secondhand furniture. She was more at home there. She let her breath out and kicked a rolled-up mattress and watched kapok dribble from its side.

'Hey missy, keep your feet to yourself,' old Arthur said. Arthur was the man who ran this part of the business. He had a boy called Jim as his assistant. They were getting things ready for the auction next day. Arthur was writing things in a book and calling numbers that Jim wrote in chalk on the items for sale. An old hand lawn-mower was no. 74, a baby's cot 75, a sideboard with borer holes in it 76.

Caroline sneezed. The kapok dust had got into her nose.

'Serves you right,' Arthur said. He was, she thought, a mean old man. He seemed to like it when other people got hurt.

She took her glasses off. The dust had made them misty. She polished them with her handkerchief. You always had to be cleaning them. Gloomily she twanged the sagging strings of a wire mattress. She looked at Arthur, and put her glasses back on. Who would want to see two of him?

She wandered among old sofas with broken springs, and radios shaped like church doorways, and washing machines with bent lids; and tables and bed-ends and sewing machines and pick axes and rolls of hose and shelves of books, and the dust made her sneeze again. Sometimes she found treasures in the oddest places. She had found an old-fashioned threepence

3

down the back of a chair and a five dollar note pinned with a safety pin to a mattress – Arthur had confiscated that – and a packet of jelly beans in the handkerchief drawer of a dressing-table, and in a book showing coloured pictures of butterflies she had found a letter in a scented envelope. *Darling*, it began, *I love you so much I feel my heart will break*. She had blushed when she read that, and Arthur had confiscated it too and stuck it in his hip pocket. Later she saw him grinning over it in the office.

She found nothing today and she was just going to climb up to the loft where the mattresses were kept when a voice said close to her ear, 'Excuse me, dear. I've got a box of books for auction. Who can I see?'

She found an old lady by her side, peering anxiously at her and holding a cardboard butter-box tied up tightly with twine and spattered with raindrops. Caroline smiled at her. She wore glasses too.

'I'll carry them,' she said.

'Oh no,' the lady smiled, 'they're very heavy. You just lead the way.'

They went along an alley between wardrobes and tallboys and Caroline pointed out Arthur, who was still writing things in his book and calling out numbers to Jim.

'Thank you,' the lady said. She went towards Arthur. The box of books was so heavy it seemed to drag her down like a lead sinker, and Caroline ran after her and helped her lower it on the floor. Arthur made no move to help.

'What you got there, lady? Not books, I hope.'

'There's some *Geographic* magazines and one or two quite nice books on railways,' the lady said.

'Huh,' grunted Arthur, 'you won't get ten cents for that lot. Let's have a look.'

4

He took out his pocket-knife and cut the twine tying up the box.

The old lady became agitated. 'Oh please don't touch them. They're neatly packed.'

'Got to see what's there, don't we?'

He turned over the magazines on top and hauled out one of the books. He looked at it sourly. 'You want to put it up as one lot?'

'Yes please. Will it be auctioned tomorrow?'

Arthur put the book back. He pushed the carton at Jim with his toe. '94. One box of books. What's your name, lady?'

'Mrs Gates,' the old lady said.

'Right.' He wrote her a slip of paper and handed it to her. Then he went back to his work. Mrs Gates did not seem to notice his rudeness. She had watched anxiously while Jim scrawled a large 94 on the box. Then she took the slip from Arthur, put it in her purse, smiled at Caroline, and walked away down the shop. Caroline went after her. She thought Mrs Gates had a friendly look, and she was ashamed of Arthur for being rude. She touched Mrs Gates's arm. 'I'm sorry,' she said.

'That's all right, dear,' Mrs Gates said. 'He's probably very kind underneath.' And she hurried on. She still seemed anxious, Caroline thought – perhaps even a little bit frightened. The shop, with its sad and used-up things, sometimes made people feel that way. She walked back to Arthur, thinking. All these beds and sofas and chairs and dressing-tables had once been new; people had brought them home proudly and polished them and arranged them in their rooms, and then they had grown old and used-up together – and the people had died. The furniture had been carted to the junk shop. She also thought about what Mrs Gates had said – Arthur kind underneath. She had sometimes thought that too.

5

'Arthur,' she said, 'can I see if there are any children's books in there?'

Arthur growled, 'Keep 'em neat. You heard what the lady said.'

She pulled the box into an alley and sat down on a stool to go through it. The *Geographic* magazines were on top. They were full of pictures of tribes with pieces of wood in their noses, and Eskimos spearing seals, and fishes swimming in coral reefs. She wished she could take them home. The colours were beautiful. Then came the train books. They did not interest her. She levered them up and peered down the side. A gleam caught her eye. Something was down there – something shiny. She squinted into the dark corner, but could not make out what it was. Carefully she squeezed her hand in and felt. There was a rattling sound. She felt pieces of wire and surfaces of glass, and a ribbon tying the things in a bundle. Then she knew. It was the glass that told her – she could feel it was a spectacle lens. Down there in the corner of the box was a bundle of spectacles.

Excitedly she lifted the train books out and put them on the floor. And there in the box they lay – ten, twenty, thirty pairs; spectacles of every sort, tied with blue ribbon into a bundle that clinked and rattled as she lifted it out. She rested it on her knee and untied the ribbon. The spectacles fell apart and spread like treasure, like jewels, over the brown cloth of her skirt. Her hands trembled with excitement. She took her own glasses off and laid them on a chair beside her.

First she picked the sparkliest pair from her knee. They had blue and red stones set along the top of their rims – just glass, she knew, but she could pretend they were sapphires and rubies. She fitted them on carefully. They were too big and slipped to the end of her nose. She pushed them back with one finger and held them in place. Then she gathered the other glasses up, laid them beside her own pair, and walked sedately to one of the wardrobes that had a full-length mirror on its door. But when she looked in she could only see a shape like a fish deep in water. Of course, the lenses were wrong. She took her finger away and the glasses slipped to the end of her nose again. That was better, she could see now – and she thought she looked beautiful, even with the glasses in that position.

'Queen Caroline,' she whispered. She posed regally. Then, with a sigh, she went back to the stool. She could never own this pair of glasses, they belonged to Mrs Gates, and tomorrow someone would buy them with the books, and that would be the last she would see of them. She put them carefully in her lap. She turned over the others, and tried them on. There were spectacles of every sort, horn-rimmed ones, and steel-rimmed ones, and fancy-rimmed ones, and ones without sides – pince-nez, she thought, another lovely word – and glasses with tinted lenses like her own, and a pair of bi-focals, and a pair of dark glasses. She tried them all on. They were all too big. And all of them seemed dull after the pair with the red and blue stones in the rims. Nobody would notice, she thought, if she kept those for herself. But she knew she would not. That would be thieving. She tried them on again. She practised sitting very straight, like a queen.

'Throw him to the crocodiles,' she said.

After a while she bundled the spectacles up and tied them tightly with the ribbon. Just for a second she saw two bundles and guiltily she put her own glasses on. She looked around to see if anyone had been watching. But Arthur and Jim were pushing boxes around, and through the bead curtain she could hear her father talking with a customer. She put the bundle in the box, said goodbye to the jewelled glasses, and laid the train books in their place. As she settled them her fingers felt something in the corner. Peering, she caught the glint of something steely. She felt more carefully, and then grinned with surprise. Another pair of glasses, pushed right into the corner, half behind books. They must have slipped out of the bundle. She eased them out and brought them into the light.

'Huh,' she said. These ones were not worth bothering with. They had a cracked lens, and thin steel rims with patches of rust on them, and sides that curled round in a half circle for the ears in an old-fashioned way. But, she saw suddenly they were a child's pair. The only child's pair in the box. And quickly she took off her own and put them on.

At once she discovered she could see properly. All the others had filled the world with blurry ghosts – ghosts of chairs and wardrobes and washing machines – but these were as good as her own. Except of course for the crack in the left-hand lens. That made a white line from the ceiling down to the floor. But everything was wonderfully bright and clear. The washing machines were white as snow, the kapok in the burst mattress looked like whipped cream, the flowers patterned on the cloth of the sofa, the dry, dusty old flowers, suddenly looked as if they were in a garden. The hoses coiled in the corner were bright orange worms; the wardrobes tall buildings in the sun; the mirrors fairy pools. Everything was brighter. Everything had a sharp clean edge. She looked at her hands. They were pink as candy floss. Her finger nails shone like jewels. Little golden hairs grew on her wrists.

These, she thought, must be special glasses. She took them off to see if they had tinted lenses – but no, the glass was ordinary, like window glass, without even a curve in it. She turned them over. So old looking, so worn-out looking. But perhaps they were magic. And she caught her breath. These might be magic glasses in disguise – the way in fairy stories princesses sometimes dressed up as beggar maids. She looked at them closely. Magic? It did not seem likely – such a cracked and rusty pair of used-up specs. She decided to test them.

She took one of the train books from the butter-box and propped it up. On the cover was a picture of a steam engine coming through a cutting. The driver was leaning out his window blowing the whistle. It was a faded old picture. The colours were bleached. The driver's face was just a blob. It was impossible to tell whether the passenger looking out the window was a little girl or an old woman.

Caroline stared at it a moment. She memorized all the browns and greys of it, the faded greens and yellows. Then she put the glasses on. At once the colours came to life, the details took sharp edges. The black little engine, trimmed with green and numbered in shining brass 275, puffed through the yellow cutting sending up clouds of cottonwool steam. The smiling, red-cheeked driver leaned from his cab. His eyes were twinkling blue. The passenger in the carriage was a girl, wearing an old-fashioned blue bonnet tied with a ribbon under her chin. She was licking an ice-cream. There was even a rabbit Caroline had not seen before, sitting on the bank with one ear pricked up and one flopping down, watching the train go by. There was a mouse in the grass, and a blue and white butterfly on a leaf. And far away, through the gap of the cutting, was a fair on a beach, children and donkeys and red and white tents, and small white waves breaking on the sand. A ship was far out at sea.

Caroline breathed deeply. She closed her eyes. That was it then. She had found herself a pair of magic glasses. They showed more than the eye could ever see.

Very carefully she took them off and put them in her pocket. She put her own glasses on. She laid the train book in its carton and pushed it back to the place where it had been. Moving slowly so as not to make Arthur suspicious, she climbed the wooden steps to the mattress loft, and crawled into her padded cave to think about what she would do next.

9

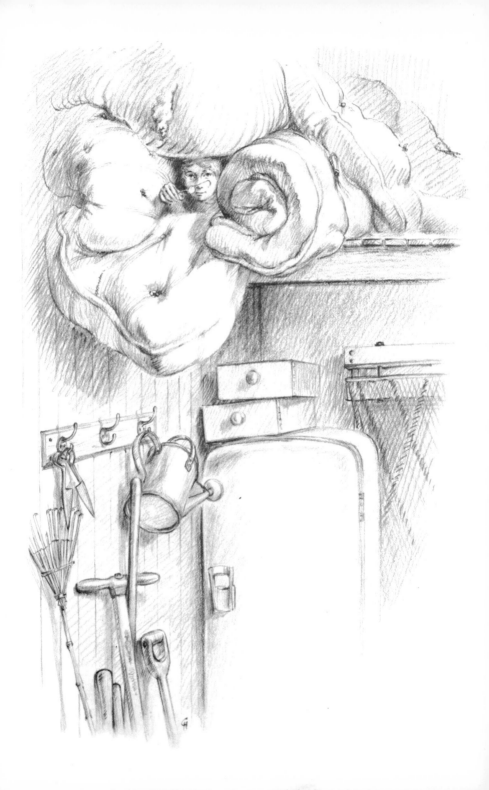

The mattress loft

The floor up there was paved with mattresses three deep, all leaking kapok and all faded and stained. Caroline did not know why Arthur kept them. They were so old and useless. No customer ever looked at them. But the loft made a marvellous playground for her, where she could do handstands and head-stands, and forward and backward rolls. And where the mattresses were stacked against the walls she had secret caves and hidey-holes.

She crawled into the largest of them. She had half-a-dozen books there and a torch to read by, and a bag of plums, and a mirror and comb set. She pulled the entrance closed behind her and crawled along in the dark to the other end. There she pushed the edge of the mattress aside, put her head out, and looked down into the shop. Arthur had gone to his office and was sitting there reading his racing paper. Jim was still pushing things about on the floor and making a noise like a shunting yard. One or two customers wandered up and down examining side-boards and refrigerators. Now and then they blinked in surprise at the dressing-table mirrors that took them unawares. Her father put his head through the bead curtain, had a quick look round, and went back again. No one looked up at the loft, where Caroline's head poked out from a crack in the piled-up mattresses. No one ever noticed her up there.

She took the magic glasses out and had a close look at them. They were still ordinary, still rusty and cracked and old-fashioned. She began to think that was one of the special things about them. After all, the specs you saw every day in the street were modern. But these had been places, these had seen things. What things? She dreamed of castles made of ivory and pearl, of flying carpets and genii and dwarfs and dragons and children lost in the woods. Then she shook herself. That was story-book stuff. These glasses in her hand were real. That was real glass, real rust, a real crack on the lens.

Carefully, with a trembling in her fingers, she put them on. The shop bloomed like a garden. Every little patch of colour among the junk and soiled furniture glowed as if the sun had suddenly struck it. Again the mirrors were fairy pools, the refrigerators gleaming icebergs. The bead curtain was a tapestry woven with jewels and through the gap in it the face of the god Shiva shone like the moon. Caroline sighed. She lay there for a long time, drinking it in. Then she took the glasses off and wrapped them in her handkerchief. She must find a case for them – a case lined with satin. She must find a place to hide them. Other people would probably want to take them away from her.

She was just going to crawl back into her cave when a man came from the front of the shop, walking in an oozy sort of way, like flowing malt. He had an oily face and puffed-out cheeks and eyes of a treacle colour, never still. They darted at every corner, poked into every drawer.

She knew at once he was after her glasses. Mrs Gates had hidden them, this man was trying to find them. She did not question it. There were things you just knew, they came to you like coloured pictures in a book you thought had only black and white ones. She drew into her cave and left herself enough room to keep him in sight. He avoided Jim, he oozed up the alleys in the furniture, looking, looking, stooping to see under chairs, pausing to lift the lids of washing machines. Caroline tightened her grip on the spectacles. She looked at the rain-spotted butter-box. When the man came round the next corner he would find it.

She wondered if she should slip out of the loft and out of the shop and get as far away as possible. Perhaps she could find Mrs Gates, find her address in the telephone book. But the rain still thundered on the iron roof. She had no coat, she would be soaked. And her mother would be here soon to pick her up. She decided she would be better where she was. No one would find her in her cave.

The man came round the end of the stacked-up chairs. He saw the butter-box. He pounced on it like a cat. Through the noise of the rain she heard his mew of triumph. His fat buttery hands worked on the train books, lifting out some, pushing others aside. He pulled out the bundle of spectacles. Caroline saw him grin. He opened his mouth as if he were going to eat them. Then quickly he sat on a chair. He began to work on the knot in the blue ribbon. But she had tied a double granny. He wouldn't get that undone in a hurry.

As the man's fingers worked her own began to twitch, and her nose began to tingle. She realized she was going to put the magic glasses on – looking at people like this oily man was one of the things they were meant for. She wriggled back into the cave and unwrapped them. Then she stopped. If the man was after them he probably knew what they looked like, so she must not let him see. She thought for a moment. Then she took her own glasses off and put the magic ones on. Grinning at her cleverness, she fitted hers over the top. She felt round the rims. Yes, her own were bigger. She had found the perfect disguise. And the magic still worked – the light at the opening in the mattresses turned from white to golden.

Caroline crept back to her vantage point. Before pushing her head out she listened carefully. The rain had died away. Single drops landed with a tinny sound on the roof. Down in

13

the shop she heard the swishing sound of Jim sweeping the floor, and a fainter sound, a rattling of spectacles. But then she heard Arthur's footsteps and his gruff voice saying, 'Hey'.

Quickly she looked out. The man was on his feet with his back to her. He was thrusting the spectacles back into the box in handfuls. She saw the flash and glitter of the jewelled pair. He pushed the books in, straightened them, and by the time Arthur was close enough to see what was happening he had the box closed and was standing innocently, with his hands folded on his stomach.

Arthur glared at him. His eyes were a bright sea-blue. Normally they were faded, almost white.

'What do you think you're playing at?'

The man bent towards him in a friendly way, almost bowing. Caroline could not see his face, but his clothes had an inky blackness, his neck and ears were yellow, and his black spiky hair stuck out from his scalp like wire. She was pleased she could not see his eyes.

'Why, my dear sir, I'm playing at nothing.' His voice was treacly. 'But trains you see are my passion. And I found this box of books . . .' He gestured at it as his voice trailed off. She could tell he was smiling. But Arthur hated being called 'sir' – and 'my dear sir' was worse.

'Well mate,' he said, 'you can just keep your meat hooks off. You want to look at things you ask at the office.'

'But surely,' the man said, and he gave a shrug.

'Surely nothing,' Arthur said. 'This stuff is up for auction. You can bid on it tomorrow, same as everyone else.'

'It would be,' the man almost whispered, 'it would be worth five dollars to me. Five dollars, immediate possession. How about it, eh? And perhaps an extra dollar for you, my good man.'

Normally Arthur would have jumped at an offer like that.

14

But 'my good man' was worse than 'my dear sir'. Much worse. Caroline almost giggled. The man must be English, she thought, a lord or something. But he wouldn't get away with talking to Arthur like that.

'We don't do business that way.'

'But surely – '

'And for another thing, I don't take bribes.'

'No offence. Oh, no offence intended. It's just that my passion for trains . . . Perhaps ten dollars?'

Arthur put his head on one side. He looked very keen suddenly. 'There's nothing in there worth ten dollars.'

'Oh not to anyone else. You're absolutely right. But to me – for my train book collection . . .'

Arthur grunted. He scratched his head. 'Well, you can leave a bid. We'll start at that tomorrow.' He took out his notebook. 'What's it going to be, five dollars or ten?'

Caroline saw the man quiver with rage. But his voice was soft and steady. 'Oh five, of course.'

'Name?'

'Grimble.'

Arthur wrote. Then he said to Jim, 'Bring me a piece of rope.' He tied the carton up. 'Put it in my office. I don't want people fooling around with it.'

Mr Grimble quivered again. 'What time will it be sold tomorrow?'

'Lot 94. Eleven o'clock. Eleven-thirty. Depends how we're going.' And Arthur walked away to his office. He sat down with his racing paper again.

Mr Grimble stood still for a very long time. Caroline guessed he was struggling with his temper – and his temper, she knew, would be a terrible thing. She drew back into her cave a little. But at last the man sighed. He drew out a gold watch from his waistcoat pocket and looked at it. Then he turned around. At once she saw his eyes. They glowed like burning coals. They were the colour of blood. They terrified her. But she could not move. The black-brown colour of his irises – the molasses colour – ordinary before, although it was ugly, had vanished entirely, and this hideous colour was in its place. She knew the man must be terribly wicked.

He saw her. For a moment she thought he was going to reach up his arm, reach up the whole three metres from the floor, and pluck her from her cave. Even then she could not move. She was paralyzed like a rabbit by a weasel. The magic glasses on her nose felt like owl's eyes. But nothing happened. The man turned away. She knew that to him she had hardly been real. Just an inquisitive child, no more important than an ant or fly. He walked away down the shop, more jerkily now, less like flowing treacle, sent one malevolent glance at Arthur, and vanished outside.

'Phew,' Caroline breathed. She scrambled into the dark and lay on her back. Her heart was beating wildly. 'What a narrow escape.' She took off her glasses, and the magic pair, and closed her eyes. 'Phew.'

Soon she heard her mother calling her. She scrambled out of the cave and down the wooden ladder. There was her mother, with her smiling brown eyes. The magic glasses would only make them kinder. No need to look. She walked beside her out to the car. Passing the office she called goodbye to Arthur. He did not hear. He had the butter-box open and was holding a tangle of spectacles in one hand and scratching his head.

Caroline smiled secretly. The pair that mattered were deep down in her pocket. She felt them with her fingers. They were safe.

CHAPTER THREE

The hut in the old-man's-beard

The rain had stopped and the summer sun had set the earth steaming.

'Mum,' Caroline said, 'can I go down to my hut?'

'You'll get soaked, dear. The trees will be all wet.'

'Just for a moment. I'll wear my plastic raincoat.'

'You'll fry in that.'

'Please.'

Her mother sighed. She put a pot of potatoes on the stove. 'All right. But don't be long. It's tea-time in half an hour.'

Caroline put on her red plastic coat and hurried out of the house. She crossed the front lawn, where the two cats, Boy and Girl, were sleeping in the shade of a lemon tree. The house was built on a steep hillside. Far below the river ran, swollen with the afternoon rain. It curved in to the bottom of the hill, then sprang out and ran tumbling down to another bend and through the town. Usually it was so clear you could see the bottom. Today it was muddy. Over on the flat land were a market garden and acres of glass-houses; then the city, the harbour, the sea, the far-away mountains. Round to the left stood a small wooded hill called Botanical Hill. A white post on its top marked the centre of New Zealand.

Caroline stopped on the edge of the lawn. She took out the magic glasses and put them on. At once the scene was bright as a stained-glass window. Wet stone gleamed on the mountains, purple cloud shadows crawled on the sea, the wood-chip piles down by the wharves were heaps of gold. The glass-houses flashed like mirrors. In the market garden she saw marrows,

cucumbers, green peppers, butter beans, and over on Botanical Hill she made out the white breasts and rainbow necks of wood pigeons feasting in the wild plum trees. The centre of New Zealand shone like a peppermint stick.

No, she thought, Mr Grimble isn't getting these. I'm the owner of these.

She crawled under the branches of the fig tree and started down the track that led to her hut. She went through fennel and a forest of barberry trees and made herself thin to edge by their thorns. Then came the old-man's-beard, the creeper that was taking over the hillside. Her father said it was a plague, but Caroline loved it. She crawled under it as though under a blanket. Here she was hidden, safe. The path went down like a chute, plunging into deep green shade. She gripped the creeper vines to keep from sliding. Then it flattened out. For a moment she came into sunlight and she stood still, while a mother and father quail and ten fluffy chicks crossed in front of her. She put out her foot and the last chick scrambled over it, chirping in panic. Caroline laughed.

She was halfway down to the river now. Ahead was her pine tree, clothed all the way to its top with old-man's-beard – a witch in a green cape and pointed hat. She plunged out of the sunlight again – another twisting chute going down into shadow. Then she was at the pine tree's trunk. Her hut was just ahead under low branches. She went towards it on her hands and knees, pushed aside the sacking door, and crawled inside. Light poured in through a little four-paned window on the far side.

Caroline wriggled out of her wet plastic coat and hung it on a nail by the door. She could just stand up in her hut, which was built of old pieces of packing case covered with tar paper. She kept it clean and neat. There was a mat on the floor, and pictures on the walls and a poster showing New Zealand native birds. In one corner was her shovel and broom and in another a box of treasures.

She crossed to the window and looked out. Beyond a bank of grass the river tumbled. Farther round, a wild plum tree grew. Its purple branches poked out of the creepers into the light. A fat wood pigeon was perched among the red fruit, greedily gobbling.

Caroline sighed with pleasure. She was always happy in the hut. She had inherited it from her brother, who was married and living in Christchurch. She knelt down and lifted the sack that covered the square hole she thought of as the back door and wriggled out into the sun. She sat with her back on the warm wooden wall and watched the river roll by. The magic glasses made it look alive – a giant snake. It would be fun to go sailing on it, she thought; and she looked at her 'boat', a black inflated inner tube from a truck, pushed for shelter into the gap between the hut and the pine trunk. She was not allowed to use it unless one of her parents was with her – and of course today with the river up it would be too dangerous.

She took the magic glasses off and studied them. They were very old, she thought, perhaps hundreds of years old. They must have passed through many hands – and they would pass through more. She did not know where the thought came from. But she knew now she was not the owner of these glasses: they were in her care, to keep for someone who needed them desperately. Mr Grimble needed them too – or *wanted* them. But they did not belong to him, she was sure of that. Her job was to keep them safe from him.

She looked over her shoulder and crawled into her hut. The thought of Mr Grimble made her shiver. She must find a hiding place he would never think of. Her box of treasures was probably best. She lifted out the shell necklace from Tahiti, the stone troll with rope hair from Sweden, her first pair of specs

20

in their case, her kaleidoscope, her red marker pen, the little prayer book that had belonged to her grandmother, with a sachet of lavender tied to its string book-mark. She laid them on the mat. But then she thought: obvious! The box was the first place anyone would look.

She thought for a while. Then she took her marker pen and the little brown case that held her first spectacles. On it she printed neatly: MAGIC GLASSES. But she did not put the magic glasses in. Instead she left her first pair in their place – a little horn-rimmed pair, scratched on their lenses and too weak for her now. She looked at them, bedded in their pink satin. Then she snapped the case shut and put it in the treasure box. She laid her treasures on top. When that was done she wrapped the magic glasses in her handkerchief. It was more important to have them properly hidden than worry about keeping them in a satin case. She lifted a corner of the mat a little way to the left-hand side of the back door. There was a broken hollow in the wood floor. (A shoot of creeper was poking through and she snapped it off.) She laid the glasses in the hollow and pressed them gently flat.

When she let the mat fall back the glasses made only a small hump, no larger than half-a-dozen others in the uneven floor. Good. At last they were safe. She felt sad at having to leave them, but easier in her mind about Mr Grimble. He was wicked, of course, but something told her he was not very clever.

Far away she heard her mother's voice calling her. She put her head out the door. 'Coming,' she yelled. She put on her coat. 'Goodbye, glasses.'

Going up was harder. She was in a sweat by the time she reached the lawn. Boy and Girl had finished their sleep and came bounding to meet her. They rubbed about her legs. She reached down to stroke them. Then she knelt and whispered in their ears, 'I've got a pair of magic glasses.' They purred as though they understood very well.

CHAPTER FOUR

Auction day

Caroline's mother worked five hours a day at the public library. She dropped Caroline off at the secondhand shop on her way past. Arthur and Jim were getting ready for the auction. Arthur was sour and Jim excited.

'We had burglars last night,' he called as Caroline came through the bead curtain from the antique department.

'Burglars?' She knew at once what they had been after. 'Was anything stolen?'

'They didn't even get inside. The police saw them in the alley. Chased 'em but they got away.'

'Cut the yacking,' Arthur said, 'and get on with your work.'

Slowly Caroline climbed to the mattress loft. It was just as well, she thought, the glasses were hidden. Mr Grimble must be desperate to get them. She was nervous. The man would be back this morning to bid for the carton. What would he do when he found the glasses were gone? It seemed to her he would understand in a flash that she had found them. It was not until she was safe in her cave, with the torch switched on, that she realized there was no way he could. Then a new fear troubled her. If she was guardian of the glasses, who was the person she was guarding them for? How would she know that person when she saw him? And would he be any better than Mr Grimble?

She crawled along her cave, poked out her head, and settled herself to watch the auction. Arthur's wife had come in to keep the records. She sat on an old wooden chair to one side of Arthur with her book and pencil ready. She gave Caroline a wave. Arthur cleared his throat and when that didn't work, picked up a hammer and banged it on a tin bucket. People came from among the furniture and stood in a knot in front of him. Caroline saw the regulars – the boarding-house keepers, the sharp-nosed bargain hunters who usually ended up buying nothing. There was no Mr Grimble. Stacked among other odds and ends was the butter-box, tied up with the neat seaman's knot that was one of Arthur's specialities.

'Right, ladies and gents, let's not waste time,' Arthur called. 'You've seen what we're offering so I'll make a start with lot 1. Lot 1, a nice rocking chair. That's it with my young friend Jimmy over there. Hold up your hand Jimmy so the folks can see you. Now what am I offered? A nice chair this. You can rock your days away . . .'

So it went on. Arthur wasted no time. His voice crackled like a machine gun, Jim chalked names on chairs, tables, tallboys, Arthur's wife made entries in her book as though she were stitching, and soon they were out of the furniture into the garden tools, and out of the garden tools into the radios and record players, and then into fridges and washing machines. Lot 40, lot 50, lot 60, lot 70. Caroline enjoyed it at first. Arthur was better than television. People came specially to watch him. But then they were into the 80s and she grew nervous. The butter-box was lot 94. In seven or eight minutes it would come up.

Suddenly she saw Mr Grimble standing quietly at the back of the crowd, with his hands folded neatly on his stomach. How had he got there? She had been watching for him but he had come like a ghost. A fat ghost though; you would never put your hand through him. She watched him nervously. His small treacle-coloured eyes were fixed on the butter-box. Only she knew their real colour was red.

Arthur sold lot 91, a set of drapes, lot 92, a record of Maori

24

songs, lot 93, a rocking horse. He took out his handkerchief and blew his nose. His eyes looked shrewdly at Mr Grimble, who never for a moment shifted his gaze from the butter-box. Arthur put his handkerchief away. His wife cracked her finger joints and winked at Caroline.

'Now,' Arthur said, 'lot 94. A bit of a surprise packet this.' He banged the butter-box with the side of his foot. The spectacles rattled, and Mr Grimble winced. 'One box of books, mostly about railway trains. Some *Geographic* magazines. And a packet of old spectacles.' He grinned at Mr Grimble. 'Now there must be some value in this lot, folks, because I've already got a bid of five dollars. Perhaps there's a rare book in there. So, we'll start at five. Any advance on five? Come on, ladies and gents, this could be the bargain of the day.'

Mr Grimble smiled secretly. His fingers played a little tattoo on his stomach. Arthur kept up his patter. But it was plain he was only playing a game, tormenting Mr Grimble. No one was going to make a higher bid. At least, that was how it must have seemed to Arthur. But suddenly a quavery voice spoke from the back of the crowd, and Arthur jerked his eyes round in surprise.

'Six dollars,' said the voice.

Caroline stretched her neck to see. Almost exactly underneath her was a little stooped old man. She saw the bald top of his head and his scrawny neck diving into his collar and his thin little ears pink with embarrassment. He was like a nervous chicken, she thought. Behind his back his hands clutched each other like a pair of lost children in the dark. She somehow could not believe he was the one her glasses were for.

Mr Grimble had shot his head round in anger. He saw the man and his mouth took an ugly sneer.

25

'Six dollars, I have. Any advance on six?' Arthur called. He was grinning.

'Seven,' said Mr Grimble.

'Eight,' said the little man.

'Nine,' said Mr Grimble.

'Ten.'

'Eleven.'

The people's heads were moving as though they were at a tennis match. Arthur put his hands on his hips and laughed. It wasn't often he got any fun from his work.

'Eleven, I have. Any advance? Eleven.'

There was silence.

Caroline was the only one in the shop to see why the little man said no more. A plump youth sidled up behind him. He looked about furtively, and Caroline saw he had a Grimble face and Grimble hands. As the little man said 'Ten' one of these yellow hands reached out and locked itself on his wrist. The little man gave a squeak but it was lost under Mr Grimble's cry of 'Eleven'. Only Caroline heard it. The two men stood side by side as though they were friends. But behind their backs one hand was hooked on the other, bending it with a terrible pressure. The little man could not move, could not make a sound. Caroline felt she could almost see the pain running up his arm.

She pulled her head back into her cave. She was trembling with fright. Should she scream? Should she run down and tell Arthur what was happening? But as she considered it, and wondered if she would be brave enough, she became aware of his voice winding up the auction.

'Eleven, eleven. I'm going to let it go. This is your last chance, folks. You could get a surprise from what's inside this box. Any advance, now? No? All right, sold then. Sold to Mr Grimble, lot 94. And that's our fun for today, ladies and gents.

Payment at the office as you go out. You can pick your goods up . . .'

Caroline put her head out of the cave. The people on the floor were milling about. Mr Grimble had picked the carton up and was walking with it to the office, where Arthur's wife was settling herself behind the cash register. The younger Grimble had vanished. And below her the little old man was standing lost, rubbing his hands. The hurt one was whiter than the other. She wanted to call out to him that it did not matter, the glasses were safe. But the other Grimble could be anywhere.

She crawled back through her cave, ran across the mattresses, and climbed down the ladder. When she reached the floor she glimpsed the man right up at the front of the shop, turning into the street. She ran, dodging between customers, and when she came on to the crowded footpath caught another glimpse of the bent little back and scrawny neck along by the public library. He was going towards Queens Gardens. In a moment she saw why. Ahead of him, marching along briskly, were Mr Grimble and the youth who had squeezed the old man's wrist. The man was shadowing them, and she was shadowing the man. It was exciting and frightening. As she went past the library she was tempted to run in and tell her mother. But she walked on boldly, and when she was past felt very pleased with herself.

The Grimbles turned into Queens Gardens. The old man scuttered along like a crab and peered round the gate after them. He vanished too. Caroline ran. Now it was her turn to peer. She saw the little man hurrying down the path towards the duck pond, where fat shiny ducks floated like a fleet of Spanish galleons. He hurried on to the bridge, looked about, then ran back and went out of sight along a path that curved round through trees towards the art gallery.

27

Caroline sped across the lawn. She slipped into the trees like a spy. Dry leaves rustled under her feet. She stood still. It was cold and spooky in the shadows. Then she saw a shape move, and stop, and move again. The little man was creeping up on something in just the way she was creeping up on him. He crouched behind a tree and looked round its trunk.

Caroline went forward cautiously. She kept away to the side of him. The leaves under her feet grew damp and soundless. A blackbird, hunting insects, flew away with a screech. Through the trees the brown water of the duckpond shone in the sun. A little breeze sent fluffy feathers rolling on it like balls. Caroline breathed softly. She slipped behind a tree with knotty roots. The old man was ten metres away, holding the trunk of his tree in both hands as he stared into a clearing in front of him.

Suddenly a voice said, 'Open it. Open it, you dummy.'

'I can't,' a second voice whined. 'The knot's too tight.'

'Here, take my knife.'

As her eyes grew used to the heavy shade she made out Mr Grimble and the youth, who was plainly his son. They were crouching over the butter-box and as Caroline watched young Grimble took his father's pocket knife, snapped it open, and sawed through the rope beside Arthur's seaman's knot. Mr Grimble pounced on the box. He tore open the flaps and threw the train books and magazines out in handfuls. When he came to the spectacles he snatched them out and held them in the air, with an odd mewing sound Caroline took to be a cry of triumph.

'That's all you know,' she whispered.

'The knife, the knife,' Mr Grimble cried. He sliced the ribbon. He spread the glasses out on the dead leaves. He hunted through them, pushing them aside like knives and forks; and finally he was scattering them far and wide with sweeps of his arms.

28

'You fool, they're not here,' he cried.

'It's not my fault,' young Grimble whined.

'Where are they then? Who's got them?'

'Perhaps they're disguised.' Young Grimble tried a pair of glasses on, threw them down, tried another pair. His father caught the idea. They snatched up the scattered glasses, fitted them on their noses, looked about; and dropped each pair with a grunt of rage. Caroline glanced at the little old man behind his tree. He looked puzzled, eager. She wanted to signal to him that everything was all right.

'They're not here.' Mr Grimble stamped the ground with rage.

'Somebody must have got them,' the young man said.

'Who? Who?'

'They were in the box. I saw the Gates woman put them in.' He grabbed the butter-box and shook it upside down.

Suddenly Mr Grimble gave a cry. 'I know. I know. It's that fat fool at the junk shop.'

'The auctioneer?'

'Come on. Get those things. We're going to see our friend.'

The young man ran about, gathering up the scattered spectacles and throwing them in the box. He started on the books.

'Leave those. They're not important.'

They pushed through the shrubbery by the asphalt path and went along by the duckpond. The ducks quacked and swam to the other side. The little man was still for a moment. Then he ran into the clearing, looked around, hunted in the dead leaves with his hands. He picked the books up, shook them, riffled their pages. Nothing! He scratched his head. Then he stacked the books at the foot of a tree. He was a neat little man. He pushed his way through the shrubs and set off after the Grimbles. Caroline followed him. She arrived at the gate in time to see the Grimbles driving away in a car shaped like a beetle. They must have had it parked there. Sitting in the back window were two fat inky-black cats. Their yellow eyes were fixed on the little man as though on a mouse. Caroline shivered. She had never seen such large cats, such hating eyes. She was glad she was not wearing the magic glasses. It would be too much to look at such eyes through those. She began to go towards the little man.

But he had already started off. He went at a shuffle, surprisingly quick. In no time at all he had reached the corner down by the river, crossed the road, and started over the footbridge. She went after him, half walking, half running. Several times she almost called out, but each time her tongue was stopped by a sudden resentment. She did not want to admit her magic glasses belonged to this man. Such a scruffy little man, so skinny and mousy, he looked as if a car back-firing would make him fall down dead. The thought made her sorry for him. And she remembered the way the cats had looked – as if they meant to pounce on him like a sparrow.

She hurried on to the footbridge. The river was still running high but its muddy colour had changed to a transparent amber. The little man turned into a path running along its side. He came to a white cottage hidden behind an eleagnus hedge and went in at a gate. Caroline approached it cautiously. She often walked home from school along the path but she could not remember seeing this cottage before. Three huge strawberry trees grew in its yard. Their cream-coloured petals were scattered on the grass right down to the river. It was, Caroline thought, a lovely little cottage. She peered in through the wooden slats of the gate. The little man was nowhere to be seen.

Suddenly she heard a rustling behind her. Two cats had come out of the hedge. For a moment she thought they were

30

Boy and Girl. They had the same lightness and quickness – but no, their colour was more golden than ginger and their furry tails stuck up like squirrels' tails.

They rubbed against her legs. She stroked them.

'Hallo. Hallo. Aren't you pretty things?'

The cats purred. One of them butted her gently on her leg.

'What is it? What do you want?'

The other cat butted her. It was a soft touch, but surprisingly firm.

'Do you want me to go in there?'

They were circling her now. And pushing her gently, firmly, towards the gate.

'All right. I'll go in.' She was nervous, but the cats were so beautiful she did not feel anything bad could happen.

'In here? Does your master live here?'

She opened the gate. The cats gave another push. She went inside on to a scoria path. The cats followed her. They pushed her along the path between beds of flowers. Petals fluttered down from the strawberry trees. And sparrows chirped and splashed in a bird-bath shaped like a scallop shell. They did not seem the least concerned by the cats. What a lovely place, Caroline thought.

But suddenly the little man jumped out from behind the hedge. He closed the gate with a bang. The cats ran to him and stood on either side. Caroline saw she'd been wrong to think him mousy. His eyes shone with a hard blue light.

'Now, little girl,' he said, 'tell me why you've been following me.'

CHAPTER FIVE

The world of Sun and Moon

He came towards her and took her by the arm. 'What is it you want? What are you after?'

'I'm not after anything,' Caroline said.

'Why did you follow me, then?'

'I like following people.'

'Tell me, little girl. It's more important than you think.'

'I don't like being called little girl. Caroline's my name. And let go my arm.'

'I'm sorry.' He let her go. 'But I must know. We have so little time.'

'Why,' said a voice, 'it's the girl from the auction rooms.'

Mrs Gates was coming along the path. She frowned. Her eyes were as clear and sharp as the man's – who, Caroline supposed, must be Mr Gates. They fixed on him. 'Did you get them?'

'No.'

'Disaster,' Mrs Gates cried. 'Disaster!'

'The Grimbles were there.'

'What are we going to do?'

'What can we do?'

'Have the Grimbles got them?'

'No. They weren't in the box.'

Mrs Gates looked at Caroline suddenly. 'This child? Why is she here? What does she know?'

'That's just what I'm finding out. But, Moon, listen. Grimble said the fat man at the auction rooms probably had them.'

Caroline listened to this carelessly. The spectacles were safe in her hut, safe as churches. The thing that interested her was Mrs Gates's name. Moon. She had never heard anything so queer.

'I suppose your name's Sun?' she said to Mr Gates.

'What? How do you know that?'

'It was a guess. Sun. Moon. See?'

'This child knows more than she says.'

'But Sun,' Mrs Gates cried, 'the fat man. If he's got them we must look. We can never give up. Moon-girl comes tomorrow.'

'Moon-girl,' Caroline said. It sounded lovely.

'We must go now. Send the child away.'

'No,' Caroline said.

'Please. Go now. We haven't time for you.'

'But,' Caroline said, 'I can help you find them.'

'What? What?' Their bright blue eyes were suddenly piercing her.

'Arthur hasn't got them.'

'Got what?'

Caroline drew a deep breath. She felt extraordinarily happy. 'Is it a pair of spectacles you're looking for? A small pair? A child's pair? They've got steel rims with rust on them and one of the lenses is cracked.'

'Yes. Yes. Spectacles.'

'Well, Arthur hasn't got them. Arthur,' she explained, 'is the fat man at the auction rooms.' She giggled. That description would make poor Arthur furious. 'He's never had them. He's never even seen them. He doesn't know a single thing about them.'

'Have you seen them, child? Where are they?'

'Please,' Mrs Gates said, 'please, Caroline. Our world will die.'

Caroline blinked. She suddenly felt very small, but she was determined.

'They're hidden,' she said.

'Hidden?'

'I've put them away. They're safe. The Grimbles will never find them.'

'You must tell us where.'

'I will. I suppose they must belong to you anyway. But first you've got to tell me what they're for.'

Mr Gates darted at her. But Mrs Gates stopped him. 'No, no, she may have saved us. Quick, get her inside. The Grimbles might come. Cats, stay here. Keep guard.'

They hurried her along the path, over the verandah, into a neatly furnished sitting-room, with vases of flowers all about and paintings of wonderful mountains and valleys and waterfalls on the walls.

'Sit down, child, sit down.'

She chose a plain chair and sat on the edge of it.

'Now tell us.'

She drew a deep breath. 'Well, I saw you bring the box into the shop, and when you'd gone I asked Arthur if I could look for any children's books in it. And I found the glasses. They're wonderful,' she sighed. 'They make everything look like fairy land. Except . . .'

'Go on.'

'Mr Grimble's eyes. They were horrible.'

'Did he see you?'

She shook her head. 'I went up to my cave.' She explained about the mattress loft. 'Then he came snooping round and he found the box. I saw his eyes . . . And then Arthur made him go away.'

'But you've still got the glasses?'

'Oh yes, I've got them. They're safe. You don't have to worry.'

'Tell us where. It's important.'

35

'They're at home. They're hidden.'

'Where?'

Caroline looked at them. They seemed kind, and terribly anxious, and the glasses after all belonged to them. But she knew adults. They always said they'd explain things, but in the end they didn't, they said wait till you're big enough. If she gave Mr and Mrs Gates the glasses they would pat her on the head and forget all about her. She would never know what the glasses were for.

She shook her head.

'Caroline?'

'No.'

'You must. You must. Our world will die.'

'I'll give them to you. I promise. But first you've got to tell me what it's about.'

'We can't. There isn't time.'

Caroline stared at them determinedly. 'If Moon-girl comes tomorrow there's plenty of time.' She was proud of herself for remembering that.

The Gateses sighed. They had been crouching over her. Now they turned away. They sat down.

'Well, Sun?' Mrs Gates said.

'Yes, Moon. We'll have to tell her.'

'She looks like a nice little girl.'

That, Caroline thought, was flattery. 'My name's Caroline,' she said. 'I don't like being called a little girl.'

'I'm sorry, Caroline. I think – ' she turned to her husband – 'I think she would have made a good Moon-girl.'

'Yes, very good. Determined.'

'What's a Moon-girl?'

Mrs Gates looked at her for a long time. 'You must promise not to tell anyone.'

36

'Not even Emily?'

'Who's Emily?'

'My best friend. She's away on holiday . . . She can keep a secret.'

Mrs Gates sighed. 'All right then. Emily. But no one else. Now I must tell it quickly, child. We have little time. We came, Sun and I, we came through the gate from another world, our world. These are paintings of it you see on the walls. A beautiful world, Caroline. Mountains, waterfalls, lovely streams, and valleys. We live in tree houses. We live on the shores of the lakes. Half this world belongs to us. It has always been so. We are – you would call us elves. No, my dear, it's no use looking. We don't have pointed ears. And the other half belongs to . . .'

'The Grimbles?'

'Yes. The Grimbles. Perhaps you would call them goblins. And they want all the world. They want our half. So every year we pass through one of the gates to hide the glasses – and also to renew them in your sun.'

Caroline blinked her eyes. 'I don't think I understand.'

'The glasses are all that save us from the Grimbles. Our magicians made them thousands of years ago. And then the secret was lost. They made the gates too. Our world is just round the corner, Caroline. And we have a thousand gates between. We come through and hide the glasses. Each year two of us are chosen – this year us – and we take the glasses through one of those gates, and so far the Grimbles have never been able to find them. But this year . . .' She shivered.

'What do the glasses do?'

'They save us, my dear. They are all that save us.'

Mrs Gates seemed overcome. She could not go on. Her husband took up the story.

37

'A chain of mountains separates the two halves of our world. The Grimbles have turned their half into a desert. They have cut down all the trees, levelled the hills, dammed up all the rivers. They live in great walled cities. Their world is one of smoke and poison and darkness. They have factories making weapons. They fight among themselves. And they have burrowed under the mountains into our half of the world. They want to turn that into desert too. That is their way. But our magicians built an invisible wall. The Grimbles can never break through it. They can only send their dragon.'

'Dragon?' Caroline said.

'Each year a dragon comes from the great ice caves beneath the mountains. He can break through the wall, he can let the Grimbles through. If he is not fought and killed our world will die. He is bred by the Grimbles, and each year he is stronger and harder to kill. And so the Moon-girl or Sun-boy we send against him must be braver and swifter.'

'Moon-girl,' Caroline whispered. 'She wears the glasses.'

'Yes.'

'Why?'

'Because the dragon is invisible. No one ever sees him except with the glasses. He cannot be fought without them.'

'Have you been a Sun-boy?'

'Yes. And my wife a Moon-girl. Many years ago when we were young.'

'Then you've seen the dragon. And killed him?'

'Yes.'

'A new one every year.'

'Yes.'

'What is he like?'

'We cannot say.'

38

'Does he have claws? Does he breathe fire?'

But the two old people had gone very pale. They shivered. 'We cannot remember. It is too terrible.'

'But each of you fought a dragon?'

They nodded.

'And killed him?'

'Yes. Some of the boys and girls do not come back. But so far the dragon has always died.'

Caroline looked at them with awe. 'What do you fight with?'

'A spear. A wooden spear tipped with glass. There is only time for one thrust.'

'And each year a new girl or boy is chosen?'

'A girl one year, a boy the next. They are always called Moon-girl and Sun-boy. They train all year for the battle. And two of us old ones pass through one of the gates and renew the glasses in the warmth of your sun. They were made here secretly and so must come back each year. And then we hide them until the time of the dragon comes round again. But the Grimbles hunt us. They never stop from hunting. They cannot enter our world but they use our gates.'

Caroline shivered.

'So you see, my dear,' the old lady said, 'why we must have the glasses.'

'Yes. Yes. I'll give them to you.'

'Without them, Caroline, the dragon will kill Moon-girl, and break through our wall, and destroy our world.'

'Oh yes, I'll get them now.'

'Wait,' Mr Gates said. He held them quiet with a raised hand. 'I've been thinking. Caroline, where are they hidden?'

'In my hut.' She described it to them. She told them how she had wrapped them in her handkerchief and put them in a hollow in the floor under the mat. 'It's safe,' she said.

'And you're sure Grimble doesn't suspect you?'

'He saw me. But he didn't take any notice.'

'Well then,' said Mr Gates, 'I think we'll leave the glasses where they are.'

'But – ' Mrs Gates said.

'Listen. Think about it. When Grimble discovers the fat man hasn't got them, he'll come here. He'll think we've tricked him. So we'll stay in the house and let him keep on thinking it. He'll send his cats in the night, but they won't find anything. Because the glasses will be in Caroline's hut. And tomorrow at noon when Moon-girl comes through the gate Caroline will take the glasses to her. Wait, there'll be no danger. Grimble and his son will be watching us.'

'Yes, I see.' Mrs Gates looked uncertain. 'But there is danger. There's always danger when Grimbles are about.'

'It's our only chance, Moon. If we bring them back here the cats will sniff them out. And Grimbles are stronger than us.'

So they agreed, and they looked at Caroline.

'Yes,' she said, 'I'll keep them. Where shall I meet Moon-girl?'

'The gate is at the place you call the centre of New Zealand.'

'On Botanical Hill? Can I see it?'

'It cannot be seen, Caroline. Only we can see, and Grimbles. And our cats, our companions. No one else can pass through.'

'Oh.' She was saddened by that. 'Do I wait up there?'

'No. Moon-girl will come down the path through the trees. You wait in the park where the path comes out. Wait on the old wooden seat. Moon-girl will come to you there at twelve o'clock. Tell her – tell her what happened. And why we couldn't be there. Give her our blessing.'

'I will.'

'Go now, child.' Mrs Gates smiled. 'Go now, Caroline.'

They came with her out to the garden. They seemed shrunken and sad. Their golden cats rubbed about their legs.

Caroline went to the gate. She waved. She ran along the grassy slope by the river and crossed the footbridge. When she looked back the little house was hidden behind the hedge and the strawberry trees.

CHAPTER SIX

Beetle, rat, cat

She spent the afternoon with her mother in the library. She pasted in book-pockets and date-due slips. But her mind was on other things and the librarian frowned at her work. Her mother took her off it and gave her a pile of circulars to stamp with the library stamp. Even that she did badly. The cats, the Grimbles, Mr and Mrs Gates, the magic glasses. And Moon-girl, especially Moon-girl. And the dragon. No wonder she could not keep her mind on her work.

Just before three o'clock her father rang up.

'Good heavens,' she heard her mother say, and 'How awful. Have they caught them?'

When she hung up Caroline said, 'What's happened, Mum?'

'Arthur McGregor had burglars. Mrs McGregor found the house all upside down when she got home.'

'Was anything stolen?'

'That's the funny thing,' her mother said.

Grimbles. Grimbles. The police would never catch them. All they had to do was hop through the gate into another world. On the drive home she stared at the top of Botanical Hill. Nothing unusual. Just trees and a patch of grass and the post marking the centre of New Zealand. She hoped Mr and Mrs Gates were still all right.

When they were home she said to her mother, 'I'm going down to my hut, Mum.'

'Enjoy yourself,' her mother said.

She went under the fig tree, through the fennel, and into the old-man's-beard. Boy and Girl followed her for a while, but ran off along the hill to hunt lizards and field mice. The chute was dry today and Caroline slid down on a flattened cardboard carton she kept there specially. She crept under the pine tree and came to her hut.

Everything was as she had left it: the treasure box, the magic glasses in their hollow under the mat. She took them out, unwrapped the handkerchief, and put them on. 'Ahh,' she sighed. Even in the deep shade in the hut, colours, colours, colours. The native birds in the poster looked as if the sun had suddenly struck them. The flowers in the faded mat bloomed like jungle orchids.

She flung open the sack on the back entrance. There was the amber river, the pigeon feasting in a purple tree hung with rubies. Oh how could she ever give these glasses away, even to Moon-girl? That made her think of the dragon, and Grimbles. She shivered. She put her own glasses on, over the magic pair, and went into the sun. There she soon got over her fright. Across the river Botanical Hill climbed into the sky. It had a million greens, a million browns. She saw every single one. On top, the gate into the other world shone like a plate of glass. She gasped. It could never be seen, but she could see it. Through the magic glasses she could see it. But – what was the use? No one from her world could ever go through. She stared at it for a long while. Then she lay back on the grass and closed her eyes.

She dreamed of goblins, and elves with wooden spears tipped with glass, and of golden cats; of a dragon that came out roaring from its cave in the mountains of ice, and of herself, a Moon-girl, wearing the magic glasses, advancing to fight it. At first she enjoyed the fantasy. But slowly, slowly, it began to terrify her. For the dragon was no dream, the dragon was real. Soon the real Moon-girl would have to fight it. She might die.

Caroline opened her eyes. Overhead were pine needles,

44

sharp green spears plunging into the sky. The sky was a pool, the deepest blue she had ever seen. She felt as if she were drowning in it. She closed her eyes again. She went over in her mind the things she must do. They were not hard: get the glasses, take them down to the park, wait on the wooden seat for Moon-girl to come. How would she know her?

Caroline smiled. She would know her.

Something banged on her glasses. She opened her eyes. She screamed. A black beetle was sitting on one of the lenses. It was huge. She saw its coal-black belly stretching from one side of the world to the other. Its dagger-sharp claws scratched on the glass only half an inch from her eye. She screamed again. She flung the glasses off. Both pairs went spinning into the grass. The beetle fell upside down into the old-man's-beard. 'Oh, oh,' Caroline cried. She panted. But she was all right. The world was suddenly real. Ordinary trees, ordinary grass, ordinary river and hills and sky. And of course ordinary beetle, wherever he was. She had seen hundreds of that sort before, kept them in jam jars and fed them on silver beet leaves.

But she knew she would never forget that coal-black shape, those coal-black claws, sitting on her eye.

After a while she got up and searched for the glasses. She found both pairs, put on her own, and wrapped the magic ones in the handkerchief. She went into the hut and put them in their hiding place under the mat.

'I'll be back tomorrow,' she whispered.

She climbed up the path to the lawn and stood in the sun. Over the river Botanical Hill stood in its cloak of green. It was difficult to believe that on top of it stood a gateway into a magic world, a gateway that shone like a sheet of plate glass, if you could only see it. She wrapped her arms round herself. Even in the sunshine she felt cold. A breeze played on her skin. Black clouds trundled up over the far-away mountains.

45

Perhaps there was going to be another storm. But she knew it was not the breeze making her cold. It was the beetle. If a beetle looked like that to her how must the dragon look to Moon-girl?

The cats ran out of the creepers and rubbed about her legs. She picked them up, one in each arm. They began to purr, rumbling like tiny engines. Holding them close to herself, warmed by their bodies, she went inside.

The clouds rolled in from the west. They towered in the sky, blotting out the sun. Lightning flashed and rain began to fall.

The beetle had tumbled among the decaying leaves of the old-man's-beard. It fell on its back but a moment's scrambling had it on its feet. It was a quick-moving beetle, flat, wide-bodied, shaped like a cockroach. It clung close to the soil until the noises made by the human had gone. Then it began to move.

It was at home among decaying leaves, in rotten wood. Two minutes scuttling brought it to Caroline's hut. It crawled up the wall and in past the hanging sack over the doorway. Its feelers waved. Here were a thousand hiding places, cracks in the timber, dark little caves and crevices.

But the beetle had not come to hide. Its feelers twitched. It stood still. Vibrations were coming to it. In a moment it slid under the mat on the floor. It went along as though oiled.

Presently it found what it was seeking. It ran over the rotting wood, wriggled in through the folds of Caroline's handkerchief, and in a moment was pressed flat on the lens of the magic glasses. This time nothing disturbed it. But it stayed only long enough to make sure. Then it turned. It wriggled free of the handkerchief, free of the mat, found the door, scuttled down the wall to the ground.

It moved with sureness and speed. It had no enemies.

46

Nothing wanted to eat a foul-tasting beetle. It ran over dead branches, under dead leaves, round roots and rocks and mountains of moss. Soon the rain came. Normally it would have looked for a dry place to shelter. But not this afternoon, not this night – for night came soon. Drops of rain splashed on its back, almost drowning it. Small torrents washed it away. But it crawled on rafts of twig and branch and held on with its spiky legs until it found a way to go forward again. It did not know where it was going, just that it had a message that must be carried. It kept on through the night and through the dawn.

The rain stopped. Down the slope, on the edge of the beetle's world, the river ran. It was brown and turbulent. Later in the morning children stood on the bridges of the town and threw down sticks and leaves and watched them whisk away.

The beetle came to the mouth of a drain. Water rushed out and tumbled down to the river. And there, high up in the dark, a rat was hidden. When it saw the beetle it scuttled out, running just clear of the water. Children on the bridge caught sight of it. They shouted and ran to fetch stones. But by the time they were back the rat was gone. The beetle's feelers had tapped a message out, and the rat was gone, up the bank, through the long grass, under hedges and over roads.

It ran along muddy drains and over concrete yards and once crossed a busy shopping street, making people jump aside and yell. It plunged down a hole at the side of an asphalt path and ran through wet tunnels under the city and came up in a yard filled with rusting car parts, and dived under a wooden wall and ran in the wet shade at the back of the gasworks and at last came to a house on rotting piles in a weedy section. There, on the back porch, a black cat slept.

The rat approached without fear. It squeaked. The cat

sprang up. And the message was passed again, in a rat language.

When it was done the cat leaped through the doorway. It skidded across the cracked lino of a dismal kitchen. There two men sat brooding at a table. The cat came between them with a giant leap. It mewed. It mewed again. The men, the Grimbles, jumped to their feet. They looked at each other. They gave a cry of rage and triumph and rushed out to their car.

CHAPTER SEVEN

Grimbles!

Caroline woke with the sun streaming through her window. She had dreamed all night: good dreams, bad dreams, one after the other, golden cats followed by black cats, dragons followed by elves, until it seemed she was laughing and crying together. In her sleep she had heard rain thundering on the roof. Now she was delighted to find the day fine. It seemed an omen.

At half past eight her father rode off to the shop on his bicycle. He rang a little while later to say the police had still not tracked down Arthur's burglar. Caroline smiled secretly about that. She knew. Wouldn't the police be surprised if she went in and told them.

She drove down to the library with her mother at ten o'clock. As they went along past the glass-houses she looked back over the market garden and river and glimpsed her hut hidden in the old-man's-beard. The glasses were there, safe. At half past eleven she would be coming for them. It seemed an exciting task and perfectly safe on this bright sunny day. The river tumbled in a brown flood, but everything else was shining, washed bright and clean. It was, she thought, a perfect morning for her meeting with Moon-girl.

She walked along from the library to the shop. Her father gave her a cloth and for almost an hour she dusted the antique furniture, the chaise-longue and the chiffonier, the captain's desk and the escritoire. Another lovely word. Her father gave her ten cents. Through the bead curtain Jim was pushing washing machines about and whistling as he worked. She peeped through. Arthur – a law unto himself, her father said – was reading his racing paper in the office. Everything seemed right with the world. But then a cloud came up. She had to tell a lie.

'Dad, I've got to do a message.' She felt a little better when she'd said it. It was not after all a whole lie – a deception more or less.

She went out into the street. It was busy today. And hot. Cars and trucks and bicycles hissed stickily through the tar. Push-chairs and prams were everywhere on the footpaths, tricycle bells went ting-a-ling, the mechanical rodeo horse outside Woolworths bucked and hummed, and on the courtyard in front of the bank boys on skateboards were practising figures of eight. Caroline hurried along past the library, past Queens Gardens, and soon left the bustle behind. She came to the river. The grassy banks sloped down to the water, the trees stood still as giants under a spell. Over on the other side the roof of the Gates's cottage shone in the sun. Caroline glimpsed a golden cat by the gate.

She did not stop. She ran over the footbridge and along past the hockey field and up another street and on to the road past the market garden and glass-houses. She saw her own house perched on the hillside, with old-man's-beard tumbling a hundred metres down to the river. The pine tree stood in its cloak. Sunlight picked out part of the wall of her hut. She saw wood pigeons in the plum tree. It was as though they were standing guard. But of course they were only there for the plums. They were greedy birds.

The road crossed the river on a one-way bridge and began to climb. It turned in a half circle. The footpath stopped. Caroline walked over to one side. This was a dangerous road. She toiled up. The sun glared off the asphalt and hurt her eyes. She took off her spectacles and polished them on her

50

handkerchief. They always got damp with sweat in weather like this. Soon she would have the magic pair again. She decided she would wear them to meet Moon-girl – wear them one last time. It seemed to her she deserved that much.

A car came up behind her. She stood over in the long grass to let it go by. Then instead of going back she climbed a little way down the bank to pick plums from a wild plum tree. The pigeons had taken the top ones but low down the branches were loaded. They weren't the nicest plums – a bit on the sour side – but she was hungry. She sat there eating. There was plenty of time.

Soon she heard another car coming up – and coming fast too. It sounded like a racing car. She crawled through the grass to look at it. She lay on the sloping bank and peered through the stalks of grass.

It was a black beetle car. A Volkswagen. It swept round the bend with a great roar. Grit flew from its wheels and stung Caroline's face. A small stone pinged on her glasses. She shrank back into the grass. But it was not the car that frightened her, it was the driver. Crouched at the wheel, with his face almost touching the windshield, was Mr Grimble.

She gripped handfuls of grass. She lay there trembling and did not dare look up. The engine roared, the tyres squealed on the curve, then the trees on the corner blocked out some of the noise. Suddenly there was silence. The car had stopped. She knew where; and she knew she must not lie hiding any longer.

She scrambled on to the road and ran to the corner. The car was drawn up at her gate, its doors gaping wide. She was just in time to see Grimble and his son vanishing down the path that led to the house. How had they known? How on earth had they known? Then she guessed. The beetle! It must have been the beetle. And that would mean they knew about the hut.

She ran to the gate. The Grimbles were out of sight.

51

Nervously she peered in the car. No cats. That was good. She could not have got past the cats. She crept down the path. Below her the roof of the house shimmered in the sun. Trees hid the lawn – a silky oak and a loquat. Beyond them she heard voices. Grimble voices. She peered through the foliage. Grimble and his son were on the lawn, staring down the slopes of old-man's-beard. Over by the lemon tree Boy and Girl, their backs arched, their tails rigid, were making angry spitting noises. The Grimble son rushed at them and they scampered under the tree.

'There must be a track,' cried the father. He began to go round the lawn, almost on all fours, peering into corners and under trees. His son took the other side. The cats came back, still arched, outraged, but not getting too close. Soon Grimble reached the fig tree. He gave a cry, plunged into the branches.

'Here it is. I'll go down. Stay and keep watch.' And he flung over his shoulder, 'Give those cats a boot.'

That was what really made Caroline angry. Boot Boy and Girl? No one was booting her cats. And no one was getting her glasses, Moon-girl's glasses.

Boldly she walked round the corner and down the path. Boy and Girl rushed to her side. The Grimble son gave a shout.

'What are you doing here?' Caroline said. 'Go away at once or I'll call the police.'

The son took a step towards her, uncertainly. He stopped. But a mewing voice cried from the fig tree, 'Get her. Quick. Lock her in the house.'

Caroline did not wait for the son to move. She had run half-a-dozen steps before he understood what she meant to do. The father was the brainy one, she thought, the son was slow as a wet week. She ran along the path at the back of the house, along past the vegetable garden and toolshed, wriggled under the fence, and started down through the sheep paddock, avoiding the barberry and thistle that grew in clumps. This was the easy way to the river. There was no creeper to tangle you up. She would clamber along the bank to the back of the hut. With luck she would beat the Grimble.

She heard the son climbing the fence. The wire strained and the posts creaked. She crouched behind a thistle and peered up the slope. He was standing stupidly, looking all about him. He did not know which way she had gone. But then a sheep saw her and lumbered away, and the Grimble, spotting the movement, started down.

Caroline crept along the slope, keeping as low as she could. In spite of the sun, the grass was still wet from the rain and soon she was soaked. But the Grimble in the old-man's-beard would be wetter. She slid down the last part of the slope and jumped out on rocks on the river bank. The water was still high and she had to move carefully. The Grimble son saw her and gave a cry. An answer sounded from deep in the old-man's-beard. Good. He was only half way down.

Caroline went quickly. Her feet were sure. The brown water surged and tumbled only inches from her toes, but she was used to this part of the river and knew exactly what to do. She knew she would make better time than the clumsy man on the slope. He was still zig-zagging down. She heard him yell as he slid into a barberry bush.

She passed the wild plum tree. Three wood pigeons cocked their heads and studied her. 'Hi,' she whispered. A fantail ducked and dived around her head. It seemed to be keeping her company. She came to the grassy slope below the hut. A sound of crashing and grunting came from above it. He was like a wild boar, she thought. And that frightened her.

She scrambled up the slope. She crouched at the back entrance. She lifted the sack aside and put her head in. It took her a moment to get used to the dark. The crashing and grunting grew louder. She reached out to turn back the mat and get the glasses. But at that moment the sack on the other side was ripped away and the Grimble appeared. They stared at each other across the tiny room. Then the Grimble moved. He must have thought she was reaching for her treasure box. He grabbed it and hugged it to himself. Then he crawled into the hut and squatted down. He tipped the box up and Caroline's treasures tumbled on the floor.

'Leave them alone,' she cried. 'They're mine.'

'Be quiet, little girl. Your game's over.'

He saw the spectacle case and snatched it up. 'Magic glasses,' he read. His hands trembled with eagerness. 'At last we have won.'

Caroline saw her chance. She stretched out her arm, turned the mat back quietly and picked up the glasses wrapped in the handkerchief. At that moment the Grimble got the case open. He gave a cry of rage.

'These are fakes.'

'Of course,' Caroline said. She smiled. 'I've got the real ones here. Goodbye.'

He dived at her. But she was too quick. She was outside again, in the sun, blinking, and his hand clawed uselessly on the grass. She looked about for a stick to hit it with. Then she saw she had no time for that. The Grimble son was clambering along the river bank. He had cut off her retreat. There was no way to go. Down-river the creepers came to the water's edge. They were a jungle. Even her brother had never made tracks in there. And the Grimble father was in the hut. His head poked out into the sun. The door was too small for him, but while he was there she could not go that way.

He said, 'We've got you, little girl. Give me the glasses.'

He looked ridiculous – like a puppet in a sideshow waiting

for balls to be lobbed into his mouth. But she did not laugh. The son yelled out. He was getting closer.

Caroline thought of Moon-girl. She thought of Mr and Mrs Gates, and the world that would die. She looked at the river. Everything depended on her, it was all up to her. It wasn't fair, she thought. But there was no use complaining.

She edged past the Grimble's hand and pulled her inner tube from its shelter. It was still blown up hard. Thank goodness for that.

Awkwardly she pulled it down to the water. She needed two hands. She took off her glasses, unwrapped the magic pair and put them on. The world of colour flashed and burned into life. The Grimble's eyes went red. Caroline put her own glasses on. She looked at the Grimble son. He was charging at her like a bull. His eyes were like fire and his skin yellow as butter. He was almost on her. She slipped the tube over her head and shoulders, pulled it down round her waist, and with a last terrified grin at the Grimbles, Caroline jumped into the swollen river.

The Grimble son gave a roar. He rushed over the rocks and reached for her. She felt a tug on her hair. Then she was free. He stood there stupidly on the river bank, holding a yellow hair ribbon in his hand.

'Missed,' she yelled; and the river whisked her away.

CHAPTER EIGHT

Moon-girl

She felt as if she were travelling in a jet boat. The tube bucked and spun and the banks whirled by until she was dizzy. She closed her eyes. This was no time to see the world coloured, flowers shining like suns and leaves like emeralds, and have the river writhing like a multi-coloured snake. She would sooner have nice quiet greens and browns.

Now and then her feet scraped over rocks. She hugged the tube tightly. If she lost her grip on it she would drown. That frightened her terribly. Just as bad was the thought that she would be swept out to sea. She would race down under the bridges of the town, and out past the ships tied up at the wharves, and past the lighthouse and through the gap between the boulder bank and Haulashore Island, and be carried out into the open sea, where, she thought, a shark would probably eat her.

She opened her eyes. She must get out of this river. She must get out before it reached the sea. Willow branches flashed by over her head. She reached for them with one hand, but the tube almost tipped over. Someone shouted. A bridge was coming up. She yelled. A boy leaned over, grinning at her. It was Kevin Smith from her class at school.

'Hi, Caroline,' he called, 'what are you doing?'

What a stupid question! 'Help,' she cried. But suddenly there was only concrete over her, she was under the bridge, and Kevin's face was gone. Then the sky flashed again, with cotton-wool clouds floating in it, and high up a silver jet making a vapour trail. What a silly time to be admiring things!

She grabbed at another branch and nearly tipped over. 'Oh, help.'

The river turned. She rushed between narrow banks hung with green glowing trees. It widened again. Then suddenly, magically, she was still. She was in a little backwater. She grabbed a branch. But she could not pull herself up. A yellow bank leaned over her and every time she tried to scramble up it she slipped back. She tried for a long time. She felt herself getting weak. But worse than that, time was passing. The Grimbles would be hunting her again. And Moon-girl would soon be at the meeting place.

There was no other way but to go on the river again. She took a good grip of the tube and pushed herself out into the current. Again she was bucked and tumbled, twisted and turned. But she kept her eyes open. She kicked her feet to stay close to the bank. The Gates's cottage went by, the strawberry trees, the footbridge. Then the tube tangled in a willow tree and she had her chance. She hauled herself free and climbed into the tree. She scrambled along a branch and jumped on to the bank and started to run. But the sound she had most feared to hear came to her ears. It roared and beat on them – the tractor sound of the Grimbles' beetle car. Suddenly it was there, round the bend, drawing up with a skid, and Mr Grimble was out of it, red-eyed, wet, dishevelled, blocking her way.

'Now, enough of your games. The glasses, please.'

He was alone. She still had a chance.

'No. They belong to Moon-girl.'

'The glasses. Quick. Before I lose my patience.'

Caroline ducked sideways. She tried to run around him, but he moved as quick as a sheep dog and blocked her path.

'You can't get away.'

He was telling the truth. This was a lonely place, the quietest on the river. No one would help her, even if she screamed. But then she caught sight of something – a flash of gold in the corner of her eye. Two flashes. The Gates's cats were speeding along the river bank, coming to help her. They ran like greyhounds, their teeth bare and their eyes glowing like suns.

Grimble saw them too late. They leaped on him, spitting, clawing. He gave a cry and flung his arms up to shield his face. Caroline saw her chance. She ran by him and reached the top of the bank. Grimble stumbled and fell. The cats kept at him, nipping his legs, scratching his hands and arms. He slid down the bank as though on a slide and splashed into the river. She watched for a moment as he pulled himself out and climbed into the willow tree.

'Thank you,' she cried to the cats. They twitched their tails and mewed. Grimble shivered in the willow tree.

'Thank you.' She turned and ran. She went past the black beetle car, which smelled like old mildewy clothes, and along a little one-way road by the river, and came out by houses in a wider street. She ran along that, seeing people pegging out their washing and babies sleeping in prams under shady trees. It made her want to shout. The world was normal, even if everything was too brightly coloured.

She crossed the road and climbed over a fence into the park. Over the grass Botanical Hill climbed into the sky. She saw the wooden seat at the foot of it, where the path came out. She could even read the words printed on it: *Bide a wee*. No one was waiting there. Perhaps she was too late. She had no idea of the time. Moon-girl might have come, and waited, and gone away again.

She searched the trees with her eyes. Helped by the magic glasses, she saw into every corner. No one was there.

Caroline sighed. She crossed the park and sat down on the seat. She took her glasses off and polished them with her fingers, but left the magic ones on. It seemed the safest place for them. She began to shiver. Her clothes were soaked from the river and clung to her skin. She closed her eyes. The colours were starting to give her a headache. Really, the world shouldn't be as bright as that. Greens and browns were better.

The midday whistle sounded at the biscuit factory. Far away, a siren blew on the wharves. Her eyes flew open. She was not too late. It was twelve o'clock exactly. And she felt a touch on her shoulder, a light touch, light as a butterfly. Close to her ear a voice said softly, 'Who are you?'

Caroline turned her head. She stood up and faced the girl – faced Moon-girl. She felt very calm, and very pleased with herself. She had done what the Gateses had asked her to do. The rest was up to someone else. But, she saw, this girl, this child, didn't look strong enough to fight a dragon, even a small one, even a baby one. She was thin, she was frail, her arms and legs looked as if they would snap at a touch. But then Caroline looked into Moon-girl's eyes, and her doubts fell away. They were green eyes, with a touch of blue and gold. They were calm and brave and strong. Nobody was going to frighten this girl. Caroline looked into her eyes as though into a pool of clear water. This girl was brave enough to challenge giant black cats, Grimbles, goblins, dragons even – anything in the world. She might look like an orphan, a waif, with her thin arms and legs, her dress of pale green, her straight black hair, her sad face – but she would take her spear and face the dragon. And probably kill him – no, slay him.

'You must be Moon-girl,' Caroline said. It sounded stupid, the sort of thing grown-ups said at parties. 'You are Moon-girl.'

'Yes. Who are you?'

'I'm Caroline. I've brought you the magic glasses.'

'Yes, I see them. Tell me what's happened, Caroline.'

So Caroline told her, racing through it. 'The Grimbles found Mr and Mrs Gates. So they hid the glasses in a box of books and I found them. I hid them in my hut. Mr and Mrs Gates asked me to bring them to you. But the Grimbles found out – it was a beetle, I think. I just got the glasses before them. I came down the river on my tube. And the cats, Mr and Mrs Gates's cats, saved me from Mr Grimble. You'd better hurry, I think. He might be coming.' But she did not take the magic glasses off. She was reluctant. All the colour would go out of the world. And Moon-girl might turn into an ordinary girl.

Suddenly she felt something rubbing her leg. It was a warm silky touch and looking down she saw a cat there. She thought it was one of the Gates's – but it was smaller, more silver in colour. It twined round her leg in a long flowing motion.

'My friend is thanking you,' Moon-girl said. 'And I thank you too. You have been very brave.'

'Well,' Caroline said, 'it was the least I could do.' That sounded stupid too. She took off the glasses and handed them to Moon-girl. 'Here. I hope you win.' And that made it sound like a tennis match or a game of marbles. She seemed to be saying everything wrong. She sighed and put her own glasses on and looked at the brown and green world. It really wasn't too bad. It was what she was used to.

'Thank you,' Moon-girl said.

'You're welcome.' She bent down and stroked the cat. She had not looked at Moon-girl yet. She was frightened of finding her ordinary. 'Do you think you'll win?' As soon as she said it she realized it was a terrible question.

'I don't know,' Moon-girl said. 'Each year the dragons have been getting bigger.'

Caroline looked at her. She had not changed, she had not become ordinary. A little of the colour was gone from her

62

dress, her skin was even paler, and her eyes no longer glowed with blue and gold. But no, she was not ordinary.

'Can I come with you?' Caroline asked.

Moon-girl smiled. She held the magic glasses tightly in her hand. 'There's no way you can pass through the gate,' she said. 'No one from your world can pass through.'

'That's not fair.'

'Things are not always fair, Caroline.'

'But I'll never know if you kill the dragon.'

'Or if he kills me – and eats up the whole of my world. Do you think you would want to see that?'

'He won't.'

'The Moon-girl, the Sun-boy, do not always survive. But always until now they have killed the dragon.'

'You will. You won't die. Please, I've got to know.'

'There is a way for you to see. You've helped us keep the glasses – so I'll help you. It will take some of my strength.'

'No. No. I don't want your strength.'

'But perhaps – ' Moon-girl smiled – 'perhaps I'll fight better if I know you are watching.' She put on the magic glasses. 'Now, Caroline.'

'No.'

'Please, I think it will help me. Take off your glasses.'

Slowly, reluctantly, Caroline took them off. It seemed dreadful to her that Moon-girl was giving away some of her strength.

'Now close your eyes.'

Caroline obeyed. At once she felt a soft touch on her eyelids. Moon-girl had laid her fingers there. She felt a tingling, a growing warmth. Something was flowing into her. Then the touch went away. Her eyes grew cool. They felt as if they had been bathed in water.

'Open them, Caroline.'

She saw Moon-girl standing in front of her. Nothing was changed.

'I can't see any difference.'

'Tonight, when you're sleeping, you will see.'

'What? You and the dragon?'

'No more questions. I must go, Caroline.'

Suddenly the cat made a spitting sound. Caroline turned and saw the Grimbles, father and son, running across the park. Their black cats bounded at their heels.

'Run. It's the Grimbles.'

Moon-girl laughed. 'Oh, I'm not scared of Grimbles. They can never catch me now I've got the magic glasses on.'

'Please go.'

'Thank you, Caroline. You've saved our world.'

She stepped into the trees, moving with the lightness of a bird. Her cat danced at her side. A flash of green, a flash of brown, a clear call like a tui note, 'goodbye,' and they were gone.

In a moment the Grimbles puffed by. They did not look at her, although their cats snarled. They plunged into the trees, smashing down foliage. They were like tanks. Caroline laughed. They could try all they liked, the Grimbles would never catch Moon-girl.

When they were out of sight, Caroline turned and ran. She went over the park, along a street, over the bridge where Kevin Smith had shouted his stupid question, and climbed up the side of the hill behind the river. She sat down and watched the top of Botanical Hill.

Soon a small green figure ran out, with a tiny silver cat-shape at its side. It stood for a moment. It seemed to look down. With the magic glasses Moon-girl would be able to see right into Caroline's eyes. Caroline smiled. She raised her hand and waved. The figure seemed to wave back. Then it turned again and ran ahead, and leaped into the air. The cat leaped with it. Caroline saw two bright flashes, as though for a second sunlight had fallen on a giant mirror. Then there was nothing. Moon-girl and her cat had gone home.

Tears began to run down Caroline's cheeks. She brushed them away. Her eyes were still cool from Moon-girl's touch. She closed them and lay back on the grassy bank and wondered what to do next. Watch for the Grimbles to go? See the thing through to its end? That was probably best. She opened her eyes. And there they were on top of Botanical Hill. The two men, the two black cats. They moved forward heavily. They were beaten. Four flashes. The Grimbles were gone.

Caroline stood up. Her glasses were wet with tears. She polished them.

CHAPTER NINE

Caroline's dream

'I gave the glasses to Moon-girl. She went through the gate.'

'Thank you, Caroline.' There was no more to say, but their smiles made her feel warm. The cats purred and rubbed around her legs. 'But you're wet, child. Come inside.'

Mrs Gates gave her lunch and ironed her dress dry.

'When are you going back?' Caroline asked.

'We don't go back.'

'Never?'

'We've been too long in your world. We can't pass through the gate again.'

'But how will you know who wins?'

They shook their heads. They were happy, Caroline knew, but seemed older and quieter. Well, she thought, perhaps tomorrow I'll have good news for them. If it was bad news she would never tell it.

She spent the time till three o'clock with her mother. At home she tidied her hut. She was angry at the mess Mr Grimble had made, and angry that her tube had been swept out to sea. But behind all this she was excited, waiting. Moon-girl's touch was on her eyes.

That night she went to bed early. Outside, thrushes were singing their evening song. They fell silent and dark came down. Caroline slept. She slept without dreaming. In the small hours a landscape floated into her mind.

There was a valley and a stream and a waterfall tumbling over mossy rocks. Slender trees with trunks mottled green and silver swayed in a breeze. Their leaves threw a light cool shade on the valley floor. Small houses perched in the branches. They were lacy and leafy, elf houses, green and blue and silver. They were empty. The elves had gone to watch Moon-girl fight the dragon.

They were gathered on a slope at the foot of black stone cliffs. Halfway up, the grass grew brown and the earth became bare. There was the invisible wall the Grimbles could not break.

Their cliffs rose up, black and terrible under a huge silver moon. The land was as bright as midday. Caves ran into the cliffs, black caves with broken mouths. A single hollow cry rang out and Grimbles boiled into the light. They formed two eager packs at the sides of the largest cave and stood there with a dreadful hush on them.

Down the slope a small figure walked out from the assembly of elves. A silver cat came at her heels. It was Moon-girl. She was dressed in a simple green smock and green moccasins, and had her hair tied with a single green ribbon. She carried a wooden spear tipped with glass. She was smiling. On her nose was a pair of spectacles, a rusty old pair with one of their lenses cracked.

She parted the wall with a wave of her hand, stepped through, and the Grimbles growled and lurched at her. She pointed her spear at them and drew a half circle in the air. They fell back.

From the central cave the hollow cry came a second time. Moon-girl waited. Her cat arched its back and spat. Then a grey wind began to blow. It beat on the wall and swirled about Moon-girl, tugging her smock, whipping her ribboned hair about her face. A low moan of grief came from the nation of elves – and the Grimbles answered with a growl. Their black cats mewed. Moon-girl smiled. She raised her spear. She

68

brushed her hair away from the magic glasses, and stepped forward to the mouth of the cave. The Grimbles pressed away.

'Come out,' Moon-girl called. The dreadful hollow cry sounded a third time. And the dragon emerged.

It was not the sort of dragon Caroline knew. It was far more terrible than a monster breathing fire. This dragon was a cloud of gas, a poisonous fog, a vapour that boiled coldly, turned and writhed and twisted on itself, and towered like a mushroom cloud out of the mouth of its cave. It would beat down the magic wall, spread poison over the valley, kill the whole world, and make it a place for Grimbles. Unless, Caroline thought, shrinking in her sleep, unless Moon-girl slew it with her spear. But how did you slay a cloud of poisonous gas?

Then she saw it was more than that, it was a thing, it was alive. Pulsing deep in the heart of it was something red. It was no larger than a tennis ball. But it was eye, heart, brain. That was the target the glass-tipped spear must find.

Moon-girl knew it too. Why was she waiting? The cloud was free of its cave and rolling towards her. Its fringes lapped about her, gathered her in. Then the cloud thickened, condensed. It took the shape of a huge black dragon, tall as a house, with paws like the trunks of trees. And Moon-girl was inside it. She searched for its heart, but the black gases surged about her face and blinded her. She stumbled this way and that, searching, searching. Her face was growing dark and strained. One breath inside that monstrous cloud was death. And the huge dragon shape padded down to the invisible wall, raised its paws, began to scratch on its surface. But Caroline had no eyes for that. It was Moon-girl she cared about, Moon-girl. She had fallen to her knees, her head was drooping, the glass-tipped spear was slipping from her hand. Her breath was gone. Caroline felt herself choking on her bed.

But then a tiny silver shape leaped from behind Moon-girl, arched its back, and spat – with the last of its breath too. And Moon-girl staggered to her feet, and took two steps through the swirling fog, and Caroline glimpsed a flash of red, a swiftly fleeing light. She saw Moon-girl raise her spear and throw it in one motion, and saw the spear fly through the swirls of gas, its glass tip shining, and saw it pierce that heart, that eye, that evil centre. And saw Moon-girl fall down stiff and cold. Dead? Dead? She could not see. For the gas had lost its shape. It was writhing like an eel and shrieking like a hurricane, and gathering blackness into itself; and now it wound into a great tornado and with a final shriek spiralled down, shrank down on itself, corkscrewed into the ground, and was lost forever.

There was a great silence. The Grimbles had fled to their caves. Moon-girl lay cold upon the ground, with her silver cat stretched across her breast.

The elves came up the hill, parted the magic curtain, laid her on a litter, and carried her down through the trees into their valley. They sang a song of victory and sadness.

The picture began to fade. Caroline struggled to hold it. She struggled to see Moon-girl's face. And just before it floated away forever, she saw pale eyelids flicker behind rusty glasses, glimpsed for an instant those wonderful eyes of blue, of green, of gold, looking into her.

Both of them smiled.

Caroline slept on, dreamless, until morning.

'Dad,' she said, 'I've got to do a message.' This time it was not even partly a lie.

'O.K. Watch the traffic,' her father said.

She went out of the shop, up the road past the library, past Queens Gardens, over the footbridge, and came to the Gates's house. The old people were sitting on the verandah.

'She won,' Caroline whispered. 'Moon-girl won.'

They were very old, they seemed to be made of paper and air and leaves.

'How did you see, Caroline?'

'She touched my eyes.'

'And the dragon's dead?'

'Yes.'

'Ah.' The old people smiled and sighed. Caroline guessed they were thinking of their battles with different dragons.

'Moon-girl's all right too.'

'Good, good.'

The cats were sleeping in their laps. They stroked them and said nothing else. They were very old, Caroline thought, much older than they had seemed, and now their task was done they were fading away. They smiled at her. She wondered if they even remembered properly who she was. Presently they closed their eyes and slept. Caroline crept away.

She walked back to town. Moon-girl, she thought – but could not see her properly. It was fading for her too. Had she dreamed it all? Were the glasses real, and Moon-girl real? And the Grimbles? She did not want to forget.

She passed Queens Gardens. Suddenly she had an idea. She ran in through the gate and across the lawn to the trees. She came to the shadowy clearing where the Grimbles had unpacked the carton of books. Mr Gates had left the books at the foot of a tree. She ran towards it. Then she stopped. She stood still and looked sadly at the place. They were not there. The books had gone. So – perhaps she had dreamed it all, dreamed Moon-girl. What had Moon-girl been like? She could not remember. She sighed and turned to go.

Then her foot struck something in the leaves. Something caught the single beam of light coming into the clearing –

something blue, something red. Caroline gave a cry. She dropped to her knees and snatched them out of their resting place. Glasses – the beautiful pair of glasses with red and blue chips of glass set in their rims, the glasses she had tried on in the shop on that day when Mrs Gates had brought in the box. It was not a dream, it was real. Suddenly everything flooded back in colour: the magic glasses, the golden cats, her voyage on the river, Moon-girl – and the Grimbles too, and their dragon and their black cats. She knew she would never forget.

She took her own glasses off and put on the coloured pair. Just for a minute. Just for once it would not hurt. Happily she walked into the town. People smiled at her.

Emily was waiting at the shop, back from her holiday.

'Where did you get – ' Emily said, but Caroline whispered, 'Shh.'

They went up to the mattress loft and settled in the cave.

'Listen,' Caroline said. She had a wonderful story for her friend.